THE Uniques

Volume 1:
Come Together
The Extended Director's Cut

Story, Art, and Lettering by
Comfort Love and Adam Withers
Background Tone Assists by: Travis Perkins and Jason Winter (Issue 2)

Color Separations by **Our Fighting Flatsmen:** Sasha, Ron Kieser, Joel Bartlett, Aimee Collier, Jason Stratton, John Wilson, Alyssa Phillips, M. Jessica Hunsberger, Marshall Day, Timothy James Hadley, Billy Miller, Danielle Prieto, John C. L. Jansen, L.A., Mark Matoc, Will Jones, Gerry Dale, Krista Schuhman, Michael Toolan, Frank Rapoza, Johnny Bourlett,

Editors: Kris Naudus, Ian Levenstein, David Jablonski
Proofing: Corinne Roberts, Tesh Silver, Will Jones, Stephen and Kathi Love

www.ComfortAndAdam.com

Wait! Read this first!

Hello and welcome to the first volume of *The Uniques*!

...Or, rather, the *second* first volume. Welcome to the Extended Director's Cut! This could probably use a little explaining, so stick with us for a moment.

See, the first issue of *The Uniques* was released in May of 2008, almost eight years ago. It was our first comic series, and our first attempt at self-publishing. The year leading up to its release was one of the most exciting, and most terrifying, of our lives. But the risk paid off; by 2010, we had completed the first "season" of the series, and had become full-time self-publishing comic creators.

For several reasons, we decided that the time was right to put *The Uniques* on hold and do another comic – *Rainbow in the Dark*. That was the book that really put us on the map. It garnered quite a few award nominations, critical and fan acclaim, and made us "names of note" in comics. (At least, to whatever extent self-publishers ever become "names of note" anywhere...) But we had never intended to abandon *The Uniques*, and as *Rainbow* neared its end we started thinking about how to relaunch this series and start work on Season 2.

The problem we had was that *Rainbow* was the book people knew us for, at that point. Since it had enjoyed wide distribution while *The Uniques* remained essentially digital-only, most people would see this as our *second* comic rather than our first. To these new eyes, unaware that the series was more than five years old by the time *Rainbow* was ending, it would be odd that the first volume of our "new" book was so much more amateurish than our "first" book was.

We intend for *The Uniques* to be a very long series – in the range of 100 issues – and so we had to get the beginning right. We decided not just to relaunch this comic, but to go back into those original issues and revamp them; elevate them to the level we were capable of, the level that the story deserved, adding back in all the little scenes we'd cut for time or space and touching up the artwork where needed to make sure that both new and old readers would get the absolute most from this second beginning.

And that's what you hold in your hands: an extended, enhanced, and more perfect version of the story we were always trying to tell. In these pages, art we created in 2008 sits right alongside art we created in 2015. Moments we always wanted to use but didn't because of deadlines, lack of skill, or because we just couldn't figure out *how*, have all come back to add more context and resonance to moments that have been here from the start. You're watching young us and now us collaborating together to do this thing better. To get it *right*.

This series is very important to us. These characters matter. We wanted – we *needed* you to feel the same, right from the start. So, for your sake, for our sake, for the sake of Telepath, Quake, Scout, and the rest... here we are again.

Thanks for joining us. Thanks to those of you who are returning with us. And try not to be too hard on 2008 Comfie and Adam when you see them peeking through the new stuff – they were doing their best.

Comfort & Adam
From their home in Grand Rapids, MI
March 11, 2016

In the year 1993...

After decades spent locked in a bitter Cold War, tensions reached a breaking point. The Soviet Union and the United States were ready to unleash weapons that would ignite a global war of epic proportions. If it had not been for a small group of Uniques, led by Mentor and Kinetic and the League of Seven, World War III would have surely come to pass.

One year later, the greatest leaders and heroes of the free world met at The United Nations for a celebration commemorating the end of the Cold War. The terrible events of that day - April 18th 1994 - would live in infamy...

Telepath
(Hope Sage)
Telepathy, Telekinesis,
Martial Artist

Kinetic
(Sue Sage)
Telepathy, Telekinesis,
Martial Artist

Mentor
(John Sage)
Telepathy, Telekinesis,
Martial Artist

Countryman III
(Shawn Redman)
Enhanced Strength
and Durability,
Expert Pugilist
and Marksman

Virtue
(Jim Gavin)
Super Strength, Flight,
Invulnerability

Speed
(Robert Flynn)
Super Speed, Enhanced
Reflexes and Durability

Celerity
(Eva Flynn)
Super Speed, Enhanced
Reflexes and Durability

Kid Quick
(Katie Flynn)
Super Speed, Enhanced
Reflexes and Durability

Motherboard
(Nikki Carter)
Typic, Highly Skilled
in Advanced Computers
and Communications

Conscience Sage
Shape-shifting and
Voice Manipulation

Ghost
(Unknown)
Gaseous Mist Form,
Expert Martial Artist,
Gadgeteer

Scout
(Unknown)
Hyper-Agility, Reflexes,
Perfect Equilibrium,
Martial Artist, Gadgeteer

Quake
(Jack)
Manipulate and Control
Earth and Rocks,
Expert Pugilist

Singe
(Jason Klyne)
Control and Project
Flames and Heat

Michael
(Michael Collins)
Winged Flight,
Reactive Immunity,
Marksman

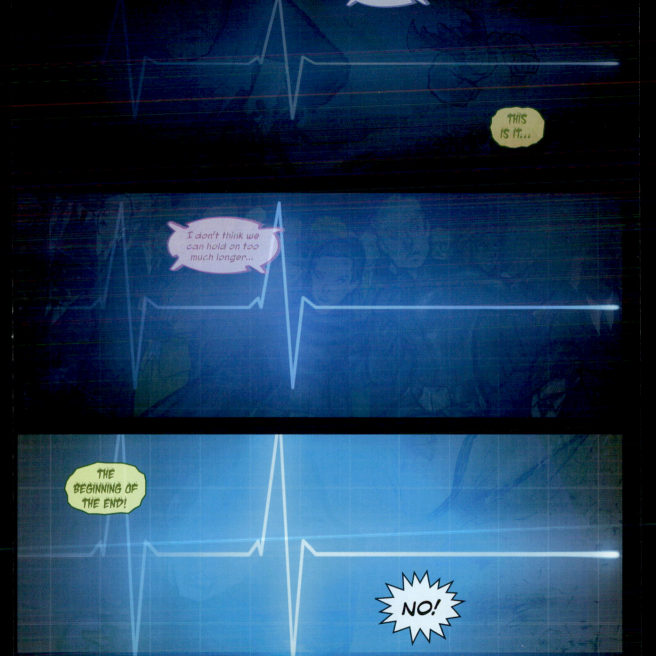

SHE IS *EXTREMELY* DANGEROUS...

Ohhhoooo That... *sucked.*

SHOULD BE CONSIDERED *HOSTILE*...

Come on, Hope...

Use your telekinesis...

You can *do* this!

AND IS TO BE *TAKEN DOWN* ON SIGHT.

Okay... Alright... Now we can--

Oh, son of a *bee!*

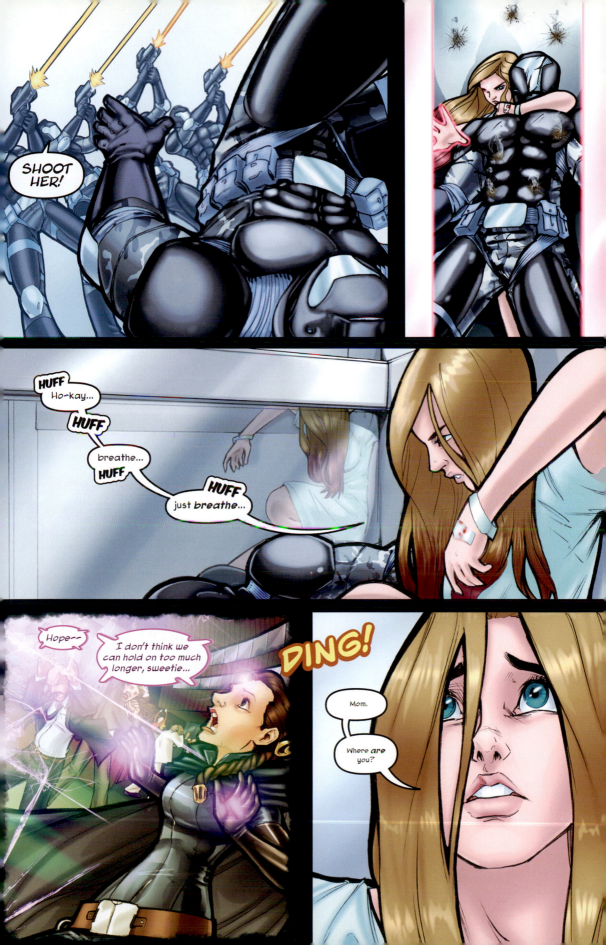

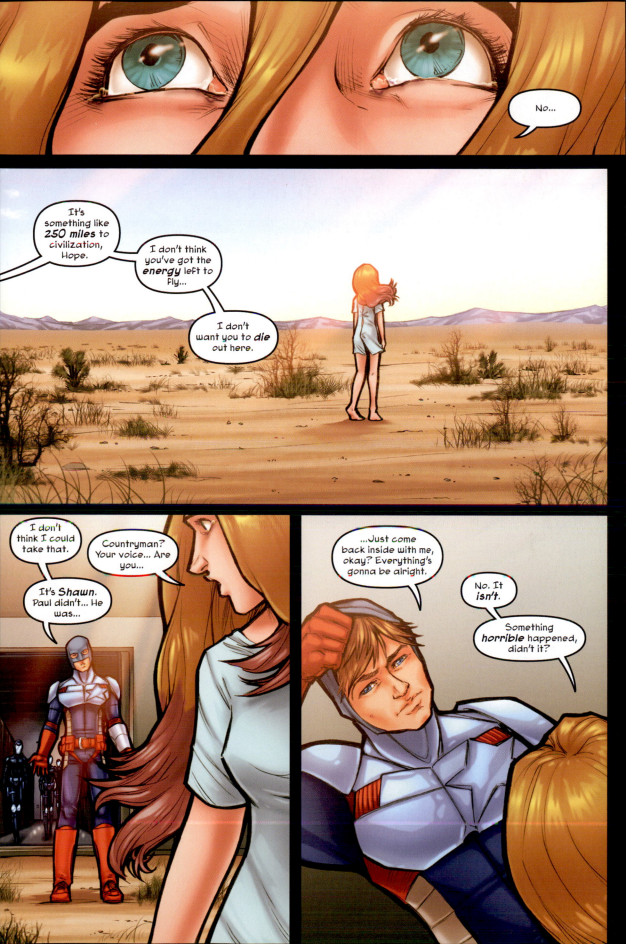

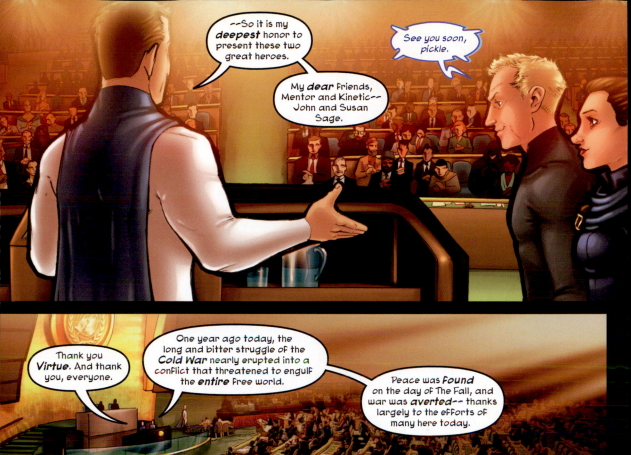

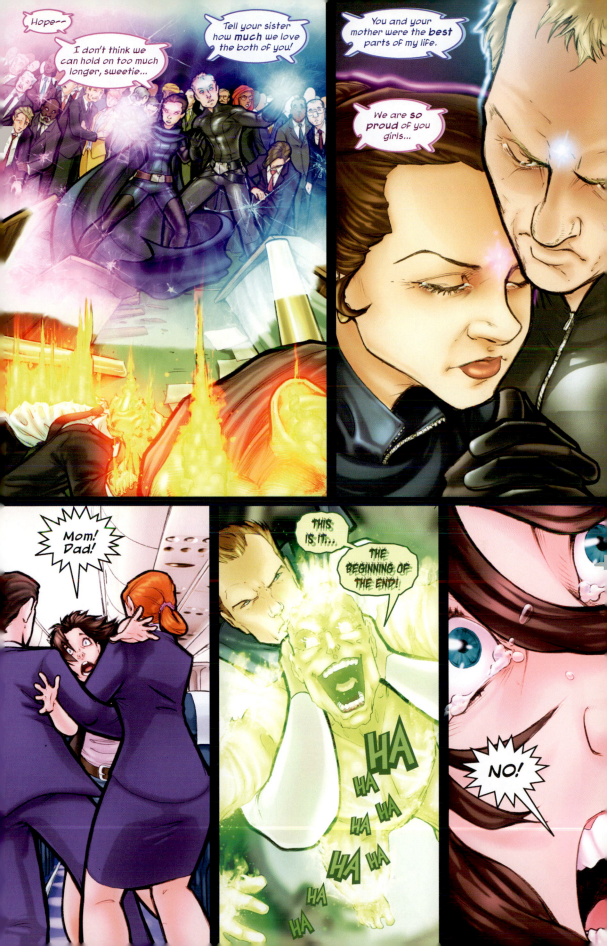

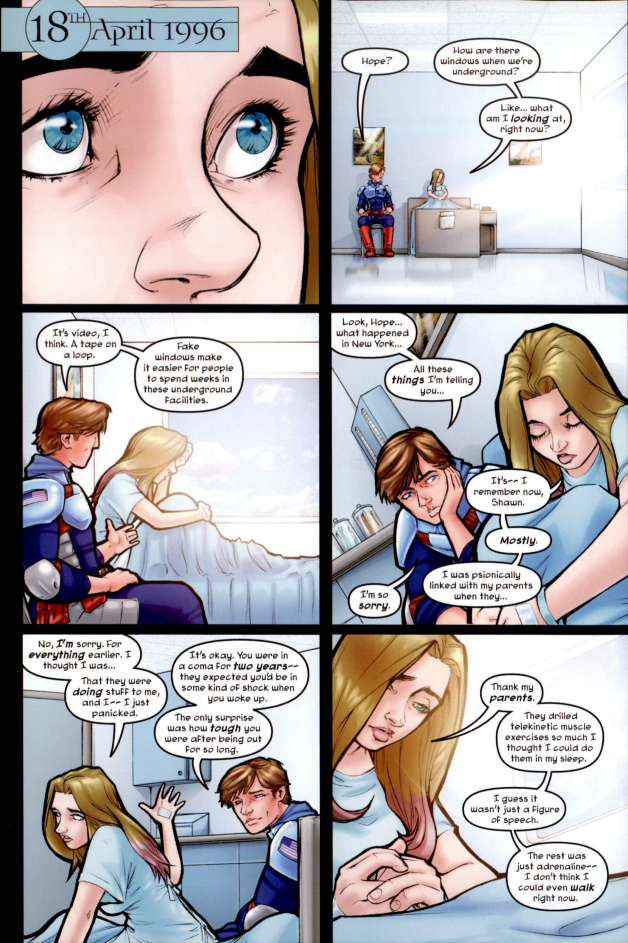

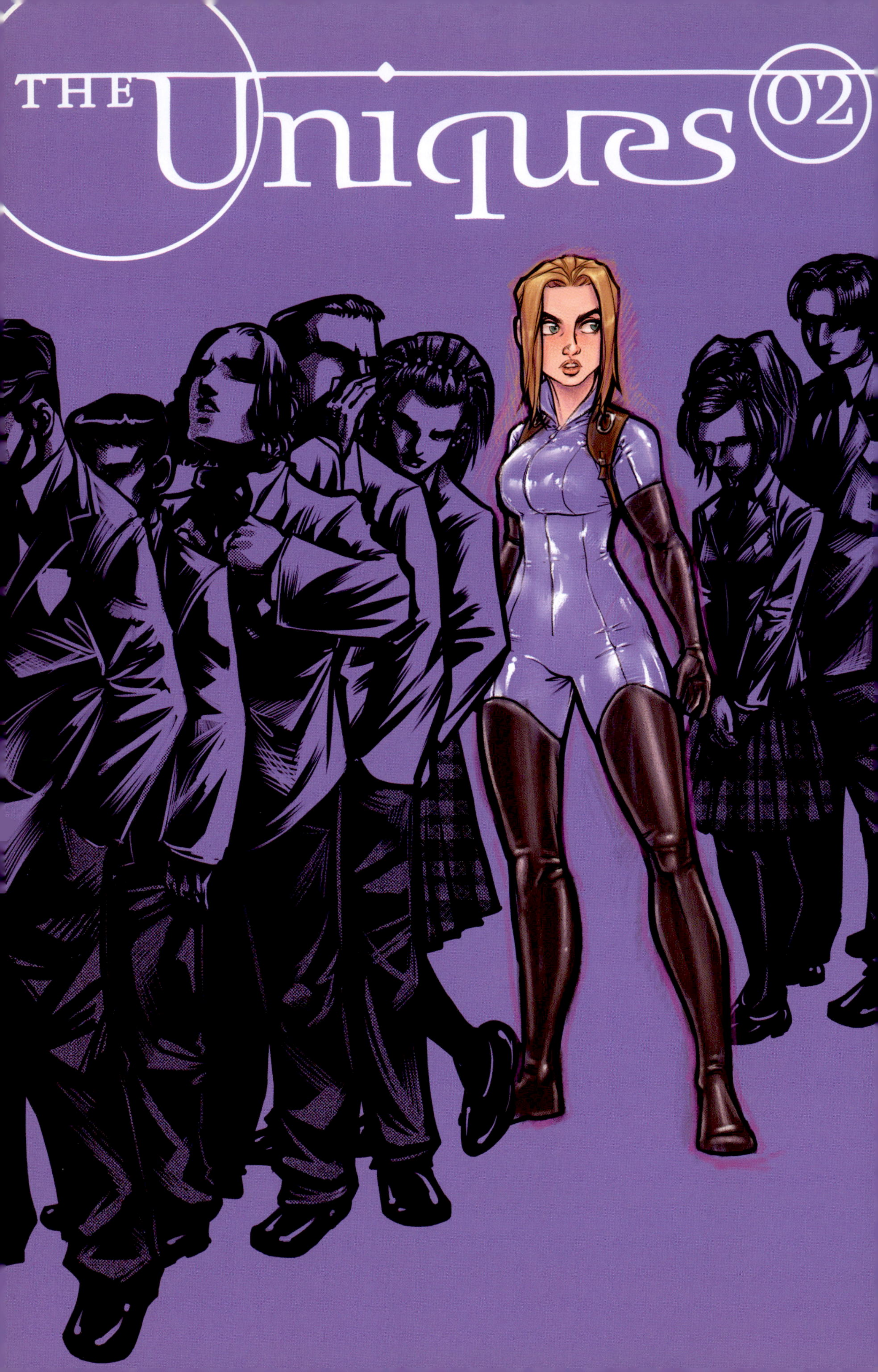
THE Uniques
02

Jim Gavin! What a nice **surprise**. Let me get you some coffee.

Ah, don't worry about it. I can only stay for a bit.

C'mon, it'll take me less than a second.

One sugar, **right?**

Thanks. So, you catch a break between the **action** today?

A **bit**. Hardly worth taking off the suit most days. Trying to make time for my girls-- Katie's inside.

With so many of us gone, I'm always--

Well, **you** know how it is.

I **do**. Have-- have you seen **Hope** recently? How's she settling in?

You could find out for **yourself**, Jim.

I... do you think she'd even **want** to see me? After her parents...

I couldn't save them, Bobby.

Any of them.

Don't **do** that to yourself, Jim. After New York, I blamed myself for Eva. I was a wreck.

Angry, sullen, no good for **anybody**. Couldn't even bring myself to **run**.

If it wasn't for **Katie**...

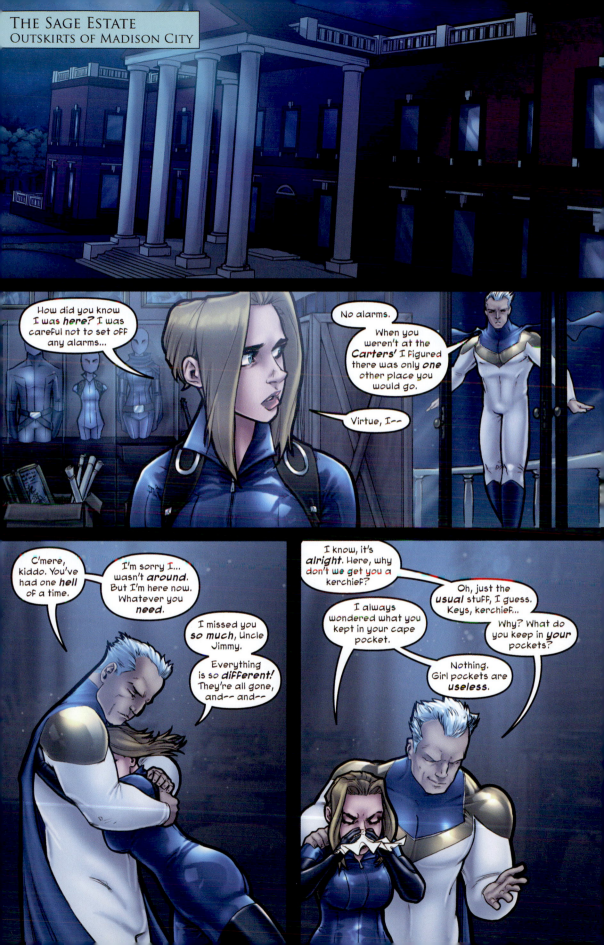

And I want to *honor* that tradition!

I'm not the little kid in that picture anymore.

Why can't I do what I've trained my *whole life* for? I'm ready!

You were born into a family that's *bigger* than just the Sages.

We're all part of a long, *proud* tradition, and--

Hope, when you were born I swore on my life I'd keep you safe.

That I'd never let what *happened* to my son happen to you.

Thank you for trying to protect me, Virtue... but I'm *not* your son.

This job-- being a *hero*, fighting the good fight...

You keep at it long enough, it will take *everything* from you. Your parents wouldn't want--

We don't really *know* what they would want, do we? Because they're *gone*.

But *I'm still here*. I belong in this uniform, Uncle Jimmy-- that's who I am.

It's all I've *ever* been. Whether you and the rest of the world likes it or *not!*

I know, kid. I know.

sigh Good luck, Telepath.

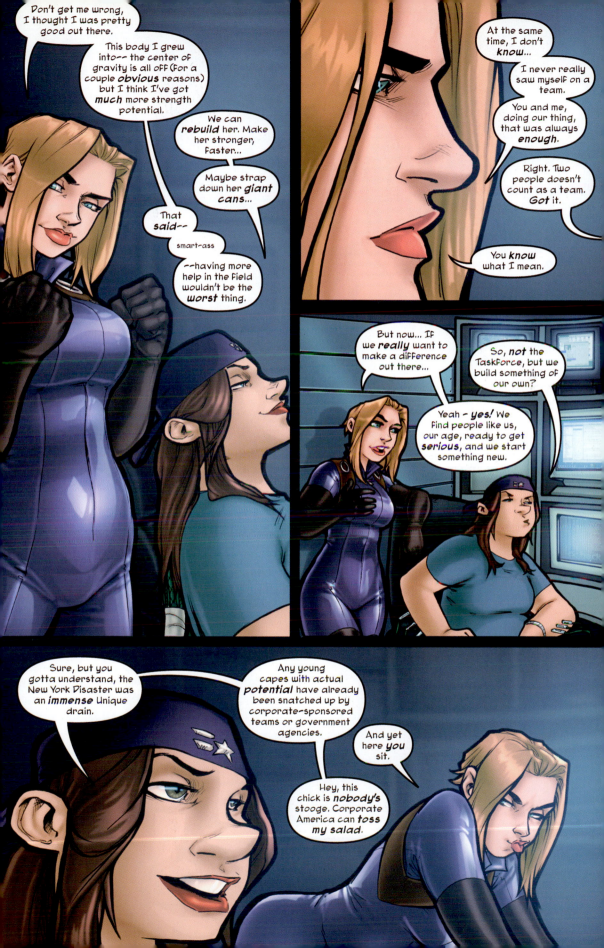

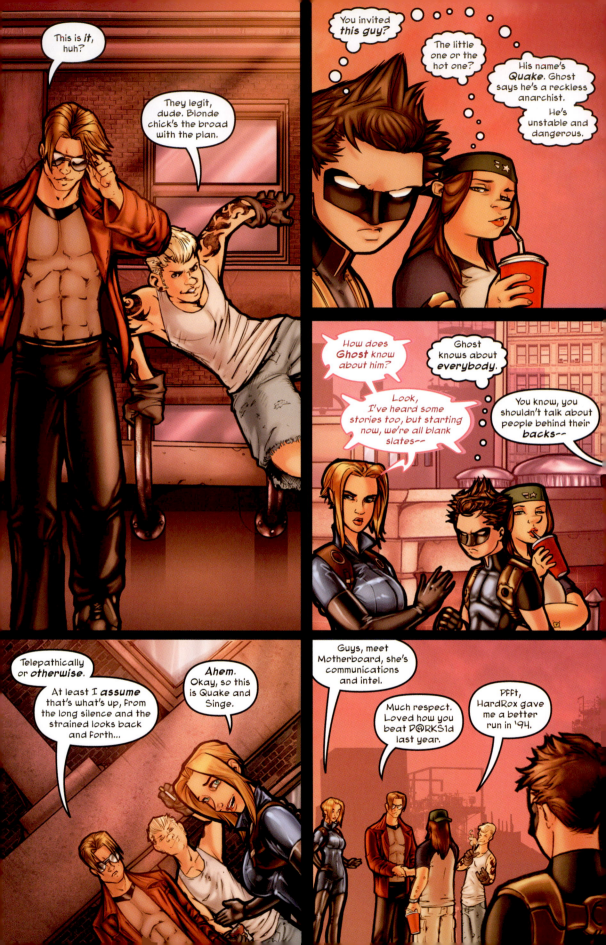

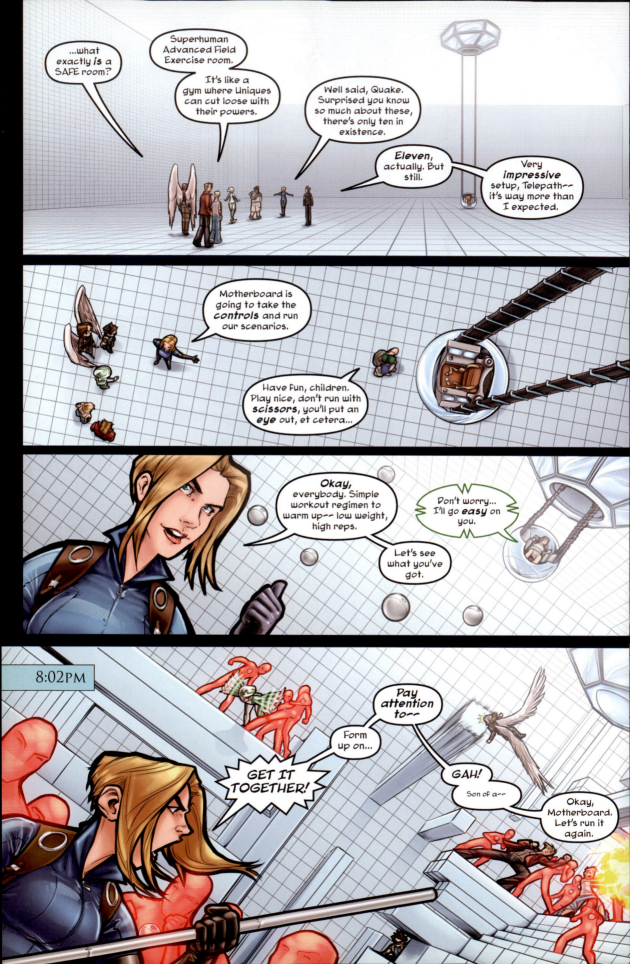

Gotcha!

Whoa! Whoa!!!

Enough, already!

WHAT?!

STOP!

Jee-zus, the hell was *that?!*

Hey, I was just doing what you-- You absolutely were *not!*

What I *wanted* you to do is use a small, *localized* quake! You almost took us *all* out!

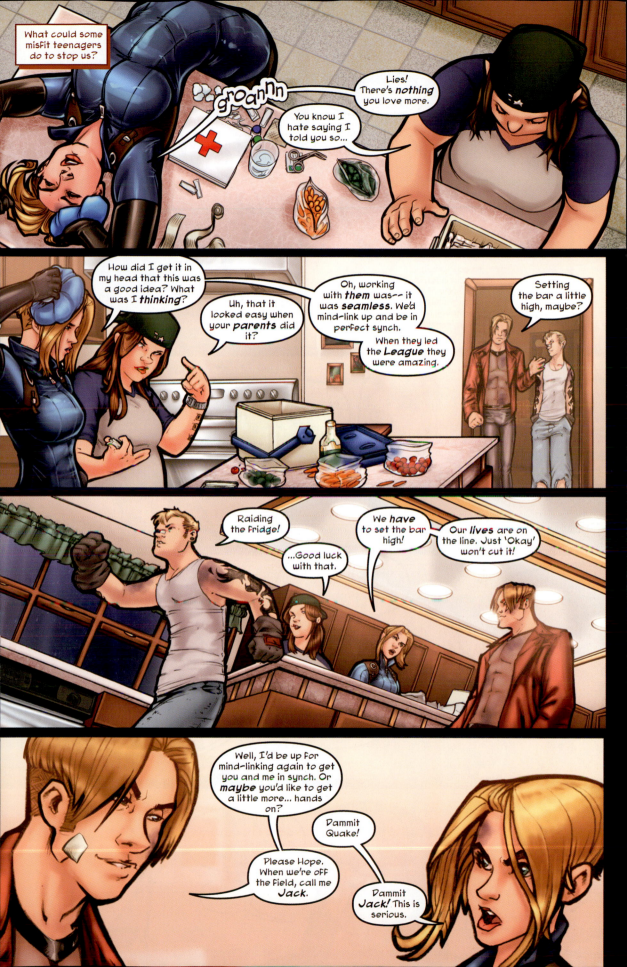

You're very kind, but this piece of art on the side of my face says *otherwise*.

So you're saying we should *Pick*-asso a better route next time?

Get it? Like "Picasso," only...

Sorry, that *sucked*. I'm not great at jokes.

It's *my* fault-- I have no idea what "Picasso" is.

So, if you don't mind me asking, how did you come to Madison?

My parents said your dad took your family to the *mountains* when he quit the League.

I was a *baby* at the time. He needed to get away from... you know, the mental noise.

He was a *Psion*.

And all the Psions... I'm *so sorry*, Michael.

I lost my dad and one of my sisters. It was *horrible*.

After that I just-- It was *complicated*. I had to leave.

You and I-- we both lost so much.

I'm happy we're *here*, now. Doing this.

Trying to make something *positive* out of our grief.

Guuuuuyyyys!

You two are taking, like, for-*ever*!

We're out of pizza and we wanna *fight* stuff!

Yeah, sure...

Let's make this happen!

WHERE ARE YOU?

RAAAAOOOOOOOO

MY FRIENDS! YES, *COME* TO ME.

ALL MY SIBLINGS ARE *DEAD*, BUT YOU AND I HAVE FOUND EACH OTHER. *YES*, WE HAVE.

THEY MADE US TO BE THEIR WEAPONS, THEN THREW US *AWAY*. THEY DID.

BUT TODAY-- *TODAY*, WE WILL MAKE THEM WISH *THEY* NEVER EXISTED!

THEIR PEOPLE WILL SUFFER LIKE *WE* DID.

THEY WILL REMEMBER THE ANNIHILGATOR.

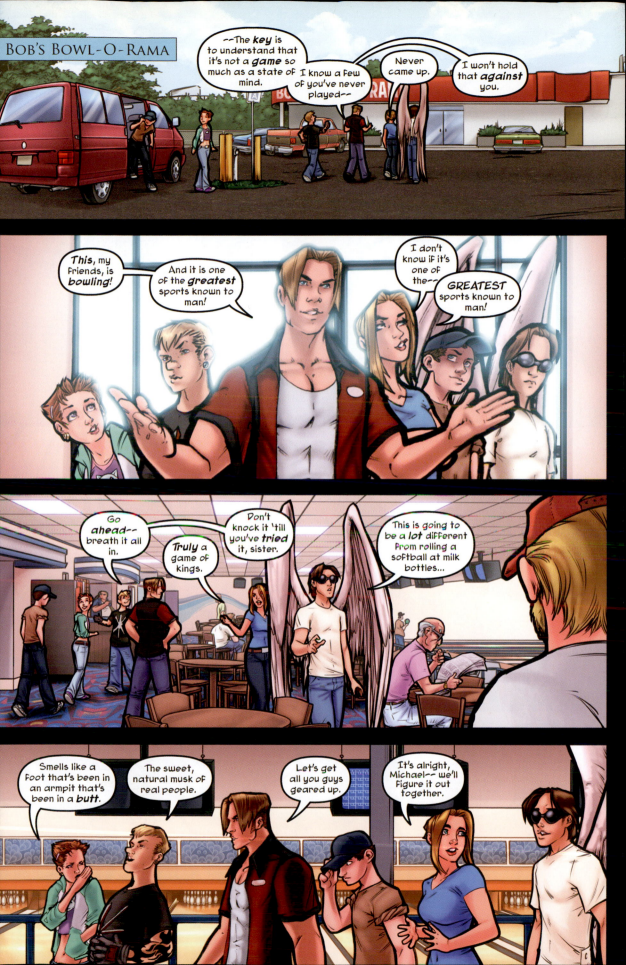

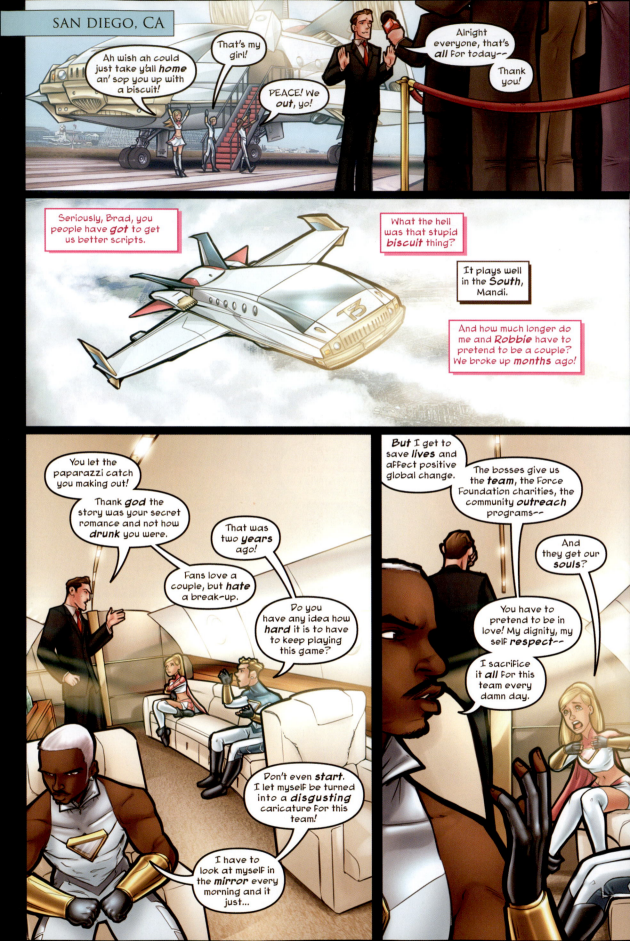

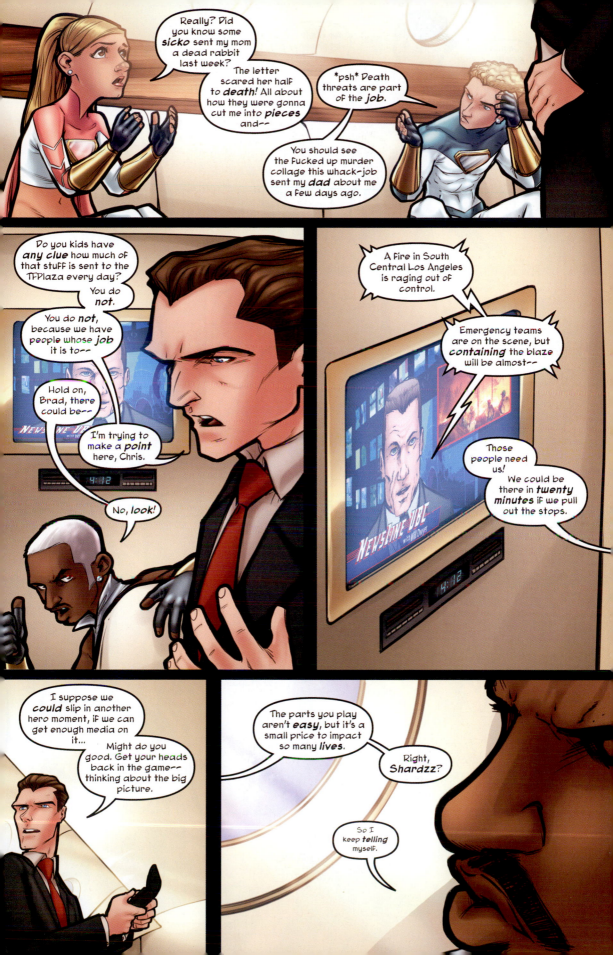

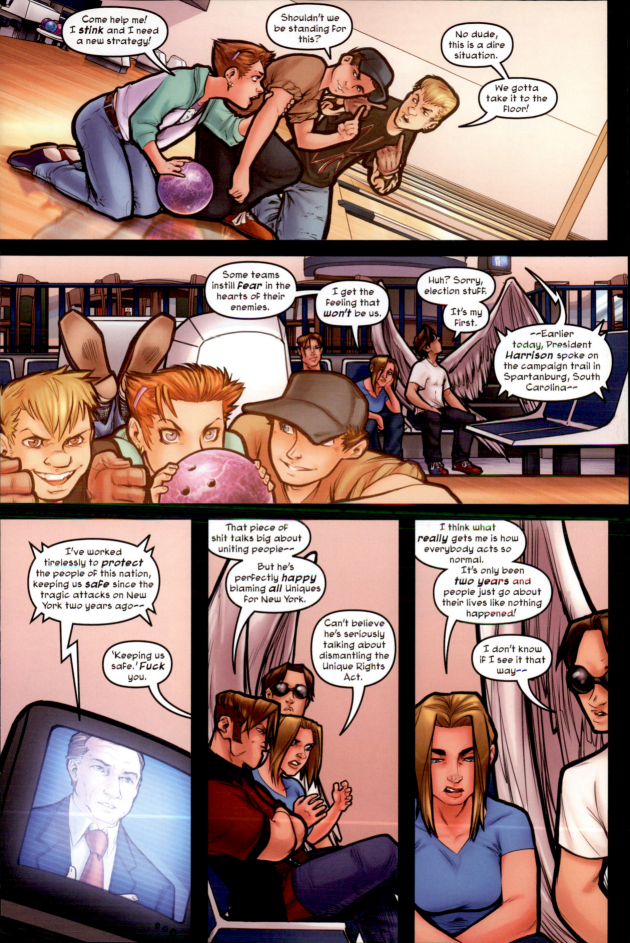

Holy shit, dude.

Nikki....?

People are advised to stay away from the city's East Side until further notice.

I *see* it.

Take over my character, Ray. I gotta jet.

That's just a couple *blocks* from here.

We could be there in *minutes*.

This is the *question*-- Are we ready to move out of the SAFE Room and make our *debut*?

Those people *need* us.

No doubt--

It's *do* or *die* time.

I WILL SHRED YOUR FLESH FROM YOUR BONES!

RAAARRGH!

Right on time!

Alright, KQ--

You're almost done clearing out all those civvies.

Thank god!

This was taking frickin' forever!

You think you've got enough energy left to back up the gang?

Against that alligator-man?

I don't know how much good I can--

Hell no! I've got a much better use for your skills...

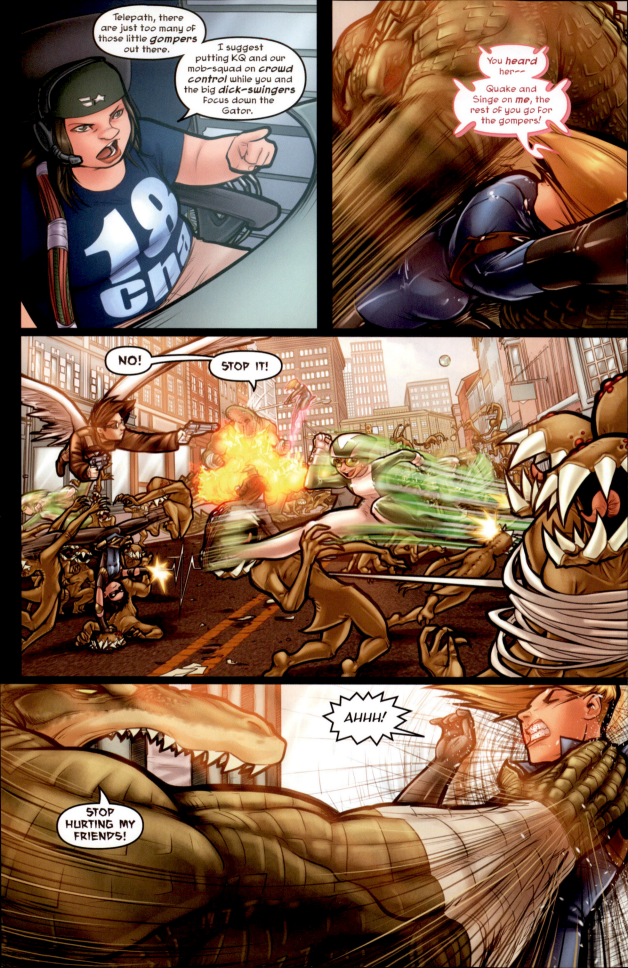

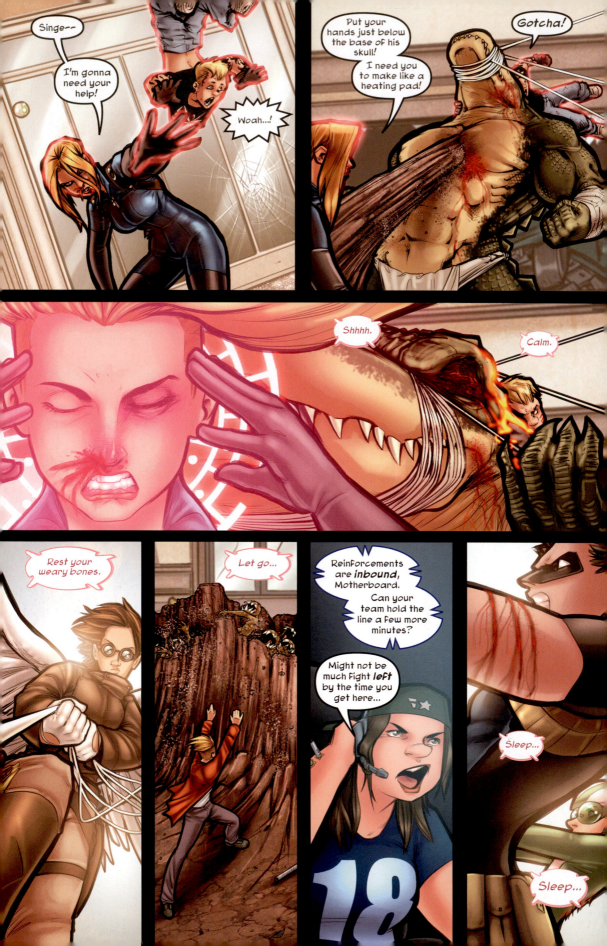

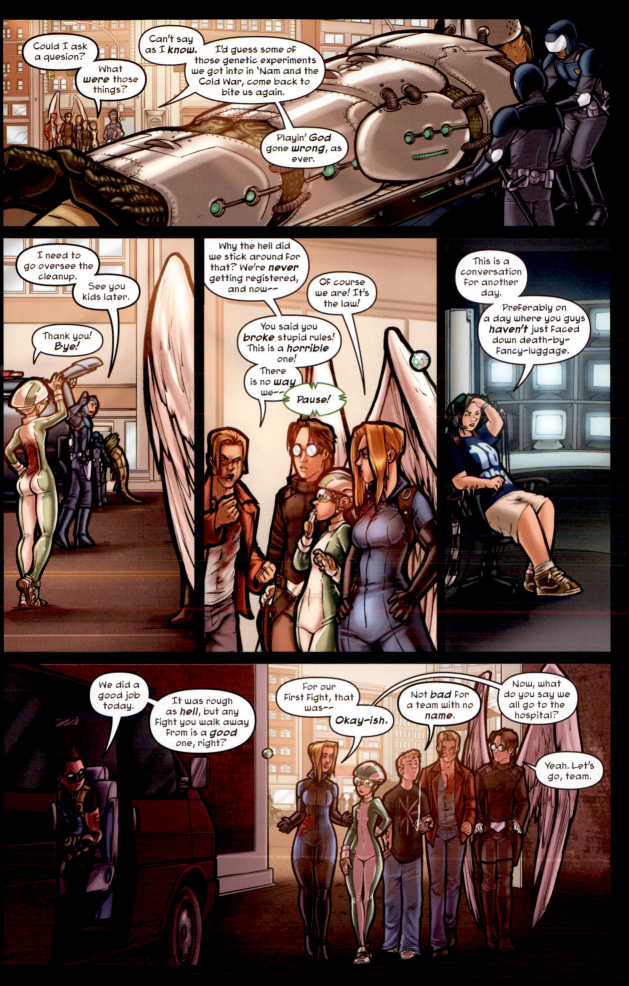

TO BE CONTINUED...

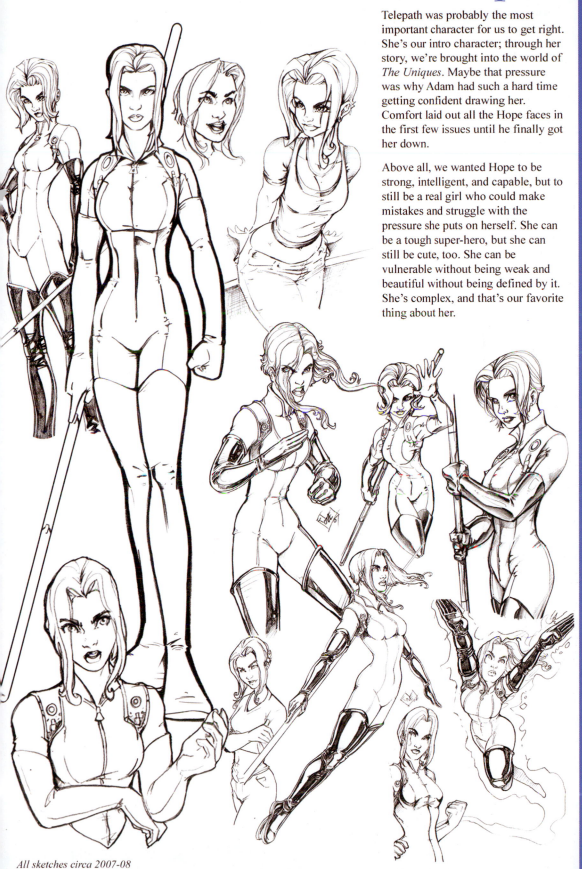

Telepath

Telepath was probably the most important character for us to get right. She's our intro character; through her story, we're brought into the world of *The Uniques*. Maybe that pressure was why Adam had such a hard time getting confident drawing her. Comfort laid out all the Hope faces in the first few issues until he finally got her down.

Above all, we wanted Hope to be strong, intelligent, and capable, but to still be a real girl who could make mistakes and struggle with the pressure she puts on herself. She can be a tough super-hero, but she can still be cute, too. She can be vulnerable without being weak and beautiful without being defined by it. She's complex, and that's our favorite thing about her.

All sketches circa 2007-08

Motherboard

Motherboard is a character you don't usually see in super-hero comics. As we've said over and over, we wanted the characters in *The Uniques* to feel like real people. Part of that means using body types usually ignored in this genre of comics.

Motherboard isn't a stereotype. Well... okay, maybe the "sarcastic computer nerd" part is, but she's more multi-dimensional than that. She puts a character type into the spotlight that you rarely see elsewhere. She's beautiful, she's brilliant, and she's got sass eight ways from Sunday. She tells it like it is and is immune to drama. She has no powers, but is never powerless. She's easily the most mature person in the room, and we love her.

All sketches circa 2007-08

Scout

We wanted Scout to feel sleek and stylish, reflecting the resources and professionalism Ghost brings to the table. We also wanted him to feel youthful without being childish. Nothing says "sidekick" like short sleeves and scruffy hair.

Our general belief is that the most iconic costumes are the ones that are the simplest. Scout epitomizes that design theory, here - even if all the gadgets, pouches, harnesses, and other gear on him make him the single most time-consuming character to draw per-panel, hands down.

All sketches circa 2007-08

Quake

Quake was another tough character to get the hang of drawing. He had to be pretty but not a pretty-boy, he had to be tough but not rugged, he had to be youthful but not too young looking - it was hard to strike the right balance.

Personality wise, his devotion to his personal philosophy and his "quest" brings a lot of momentum to the team, but also creates conflict. He's a real Alpha personality, and that clashes with all the other Alphas in the team (most notably Telepath).

Quake's progression through the story, revealing his character to be something deeper and more nuanced than a simple bad-boy womanizer, has been one of our favorite parts of making this comic. He's definitely a character to watch.

All sketches circa 2007-08

Singe

Ah, Singe. There isn't much to say about him, artistically. He sprang almost fully formed out of our earliest sketches. The trick was balancing the boyishness with the street-tough side of him. His expressions are some of the most fun things to draw in the whole book.

The tattoos were a little tricky, as they required us to find something detailed yet easy to draw over and over. A bit of tat research found us all the pieces we needed.

Oh, and those pants of his? The ones with the huge holes in the knees? They really exist. A friend of ours owns them, and we thought they'd be perfect for Singe. They tell you so much about him in one simple shot.

All sketches circa 2007-08

Kid Quick

When we started Katie's design, we knew two things: she was her parents' sidekick and her costume should reflect that, and we wanted her to have a very different feel from the other two girls on the team. All three needed to stand apart from each other.

The costume is a streamlined version of her parents' (Speed and Celerity). We added the helmet because we figured they would make her wear one (for safety!). Comfort originally had her dressed in red and white, but we changed it to green to avoid similarities with other speedster heroes, and because her parents wore yellow and blue. As any artist would tell you, if you combine the colors yellow and blue, you get green. Yay, art school joke!

All sketches circa 2007-08

Michael

With Michael, we really wanted to push away from anything overtly angelic. We took a guy with wings and made him a retro gunslinger. Equal parts Han Solo and the Rocketeer, he has that WWII feel that we found instantly appealing. The pistols use alien tech but are based on old-fashioned revolvers for a bit of wild-west flair.

As a character, he's very quiet and introspective. This is really his first foray into social interaction with people his own age, and he isn't confident enough or familiar enough to assert himself yet. He's getting there, but with Michael you have to look closely at his body language and when he chooses to speak. In this first season, a lot of his characterization is still in the subtext.

All sketches circa 2007-08

THE Uniques
Then and Now

The entire concept of doing a "Director's Cut" comic is unusual. If asked, we would recommend against it almost every time. But there were reasons we felt that, after leaving the book for several years to produce *Rainbow in the Dark* and *The Complete Guide to Self Publishing*, the only way to move forward with *The Uniques* was to first go back to the beginning.

Our favorite stories are those where the seeds of the ending are planted from the very first chapter; where you can finish the story and then go all the way back to the beginning and find that there are scenes telegraphing the finale that you never noticed before. The whole tale changes and you appreciate the full arc

Comfort and Adam on the convention trail in 2008

But that only works if the first chapters stand strong on their own. *The Uniques* had been our first serious comics work, and we had a lot to learn. We might not have been ready for this epic when we released the first issue in 2008, but we've come a long way and we're definitely ready now.

The following pages show the kinds of additions and enhancements we went through to elevate the '08-09 *Uniques,* relaunching the series with a higher standard of quality in aesthetics and storytelling.

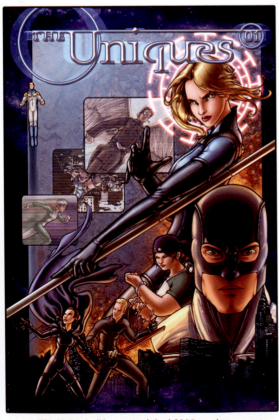

The Uniques #1 cover, original 2008 version

The Uniques Extended Directors' Cut #1 cover, 2015

Page Flow: Fewer Panels Per Page

The biggest issue with the early chapters of *The Uniques* was that we were trying to squeeze too much story into too little space.

A fear all self-publishers have to contend with is the question of how long you can keep yourself going. We were nervous about how long we'd last on our own, and so felt pressure to hurry the story along and "get to the good stuff" as fast as possible. That meant cramming a lot of content in early and rushing the plot.

Now that we know we'll be fine and can keep this train running, the first thing we wanted to do was to open up these early scenes and give the panels more room to breathe. That was one of the primary goals of the *Expanded Directors' Cut* (EDC).

Panel count matters. More panels means smaller panels, and smaller panels can feel less significant than larger ones and more claustrophobic. Fewer panels gives more room for the art to show, more room for dialogue, and feels less cramped overall.

That dialogue thing matters - we're willing to make *The Uniques* a fairly talky book. We believe in the power of dialogue to create character and bond the audience to the cast, but you can't have both a lot of dialogue *and* a lot of panels on every page. If we had to pick one, we prefer more pages per scene with more space to read and enjoy the pictures on each page.

Top: The opening page of the hospital sequence from The Uniques #1 (2008)
Right: *The same page re-worked for the EDC (2015)*

Page Flow: Expanding Scenes

Top: *The second of only two pages covering the entire U.N. fight from The Uniques #1 (2008). While we were trying to create an interesting rhythm to the panels here, the composition is simply too tight and panels too small to create the impact we wanted.*

Right: *The same content now stretches across three full pages in the EDC (2015).*

Rushing the early issues didn't just mean using too many panels, it also often meant that important scenes were glossed over too quickly. The EDC was an opportunity to go into those scenes and expand them.

The U.N. attack from issue #1 is a great example of this. It's the inciting incident for the entire series, and the defining moment for many of the main cast, but it was all but glossed over in its original presentation. We felt it was important to give it more space if only to spend more time with Telepath's parents and get a better sense of that terrible event.

It also enhances the story, making Kiloton's actions more clear - including the fact that he wasn't acting alone, which was an important fact glossed over in the original.

In the end, so many scenes were expanded in this way, either for pacing, panel count, or story reasons, that the original first issue of *The Uniques* became the first two issues of the EDC release! Several more scenes throughout the EDC got this treatment as well, including the SAFE Room training sequences, the bowling scene, and the Annihilgator fight.

Refurbished Panels

The most obvious changes we made for the EDC were purely aesthetic - we wanted the art to look better. This is where our many years of experience and growth while making comics was both a problem and a solution.

The problem was, if we started up *The Uniques* again to continue the series after a years-long hiatus, the art just wouldn't match at all. That's a big issue for a series as intricately interwoven as this.

The solution was simply to go in and sweeten the old art, refining panels here, redoing them there, so it would all come together more naturally.

This required a cautious approach, because our new art was going to look really out of place next to panels from 7 years ago.

When refurbishing panels, we had to carefully weigh the stylistic differences between then and now, trying our best to find a good balance where the old art didn't feel too radically out of place.

We know it's a balance that isn't perfect, but we think you'd be surprised how often little details of characters or backgrounds, color, texture, or special effects have been enhanced, refurbished, or completely redone. For every one you spot, there are probably several more too seamless to recognize.

...At least, that's what we *hope*.

Top: *Panel comparisons from The Uniques #2 (2008) and the EDC #3 (2015)*
Bottom: *Panel comparisons from The Uniques #3 (2008) and the EDC #4 (2015)*

New Establishing Shots

Establishing shots are extremely important in comics storytelling. In one panel, you see where the characters are, who is present, what they're doing, and a host of other valuable facts.

A major goal for the EDC was going back in and either enhancing existing establishing shots, or adding them where we simply hadn't realized they were needed before.

Top: Two new establishing shots from the EDC #4 better set the scene for the Annihilgator fight and the bowling alley. (2015)
Bottom: Compare the original shot of the Sage Estate from The Uniques #1 (2008) to the new shot from the EDC #2 (2015)

Script and Lettering

The tradeoff to writing dialogue-heavy comics is that you have to find a way to avoid clogging up the page with text. Our writing and lettering skills have vastly improved, and we used our new abilities to not only reduce text by saying things in fewer words, but to reduce clutter with better balloon placement.

Above: Original page from *The Uniques #1* (2008)

We remain deeply committed to doing our best to write characters who talk like normal people, but that shouldn't require asking the reader to sit through a novel every issue. Sometimes you really can do more with less, and we're working harder to find that balance.

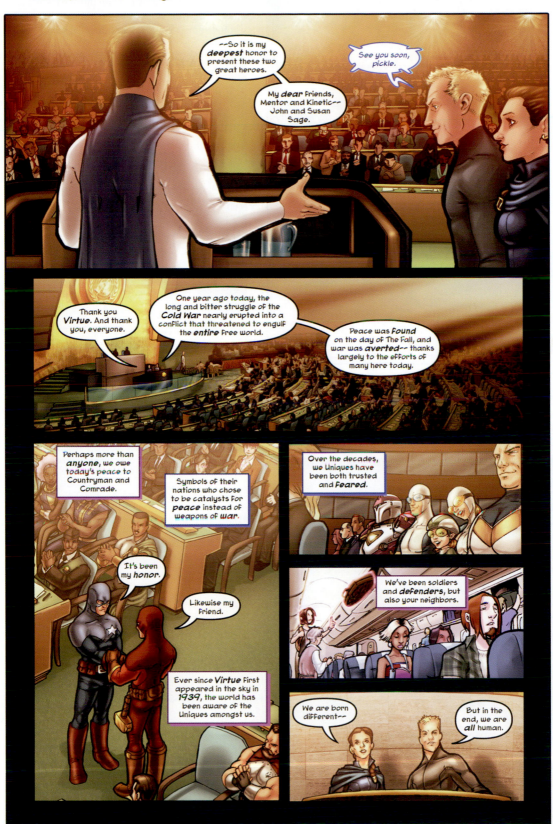

Above: Refurbished page from the UDC (2015)

A More Unique World

We made a number of changes to help differentiate our world. When we put out The Uniques #1 in 2008, the Skycarrier was a fun throwback idea. Since then, with Helicarriers in the movies, we wanted something that wouldn't feel so derivative.

We love our archetypal characters, but we wanted to ensure they were more clearly their own people. This led to some changes like Ghost's Tomb becoming an underwater lair - cold and detached in a less obvious sort of way from a cave.

Re-Imagined Scenes

Some scenes we liked, but felt needed a different approach, such as Telepath's conversataions with Virtue and Countryman in EDC #2. In the first, the trophy room was a way to show her surrounded by an unfinished life she couldn't get back, while being less on-the-nose than the memorial stone for her dead parents. The second benefitted from a more visual approach to her telepathy and a more open environment that continued from a fight that was more fleshed out than the original, serving a bigger purpose in the story.

Top: The Virtue talk from *The Uniques #1* (left, 2008) and the EDC #2 (right, 2015)
Bottom: The Countryman talk from *The Uniques #1* (left, 2008) and the EDC #2 (right, 2015)

Expanding the Story

18th April 1994
The United Nations
New York City

Perhaps the most valuable additions to the EDC were the brand-new scenes we added. In our rush to get the initial issues finished and released in 2008, there was a lot of material left on the cutting-room floor (so to speak). Several scenes we really liked just never found a home because we were so anxious to get to the "meat" of the story.

The EDC was our chance to bring those story beats back. So now we get to actually see the ruination of New York City through Virtue's eyes, a moment that drives most of his actions in the rest of the series. We get to see Hope trying (and failing) to live a normal life, and that Motherboard's family are the ones who take her in and give her a home.

We get more time with characters like Conscience and Countryman, both of whom will only become more important as the series continues. And we get more glimpses into the lives of the main cast, getting a more rounded idea of where they are and what their lives are like when the series begins.

Left and Below: Virtue wakes up in the ruins of New York City - the only survivor from ground zero. EDC #2 (2015)

These new scenes also allowed us to hone in on elements of the series that had never really been addressed before. A good example is EDC #2, the only issue comprised of nothing but new content.

The series had always presented that these characters came together as a team and stayed together because there were things missing in their lives that only being part of the team could fix. And yet we never actually showed what those things were! The new second issue gave us the chance to explain where each of the characters were at and in which ways they were all missing something important to them.

So now we can experience Scout's loneliness, Kid Quick's need to feel useful and appreciated, Quake's drive to take his quest for social change to another level and Singe's desire for a home. We get to see Telepath and Motherboard trying to get back into their old routine, and then see the ways it falls short of what they really want to accomplish.

These were all things we'd wanted to do initially, but didn't feel we had the time to tackle. Now we do, and the series is stronger for it.

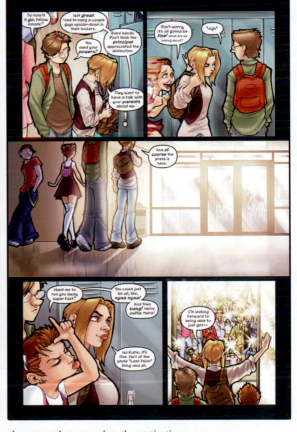

Above: The most important new material are the scenes that expand on the motivations and drives of the main characters. From EDC #2 (2015)

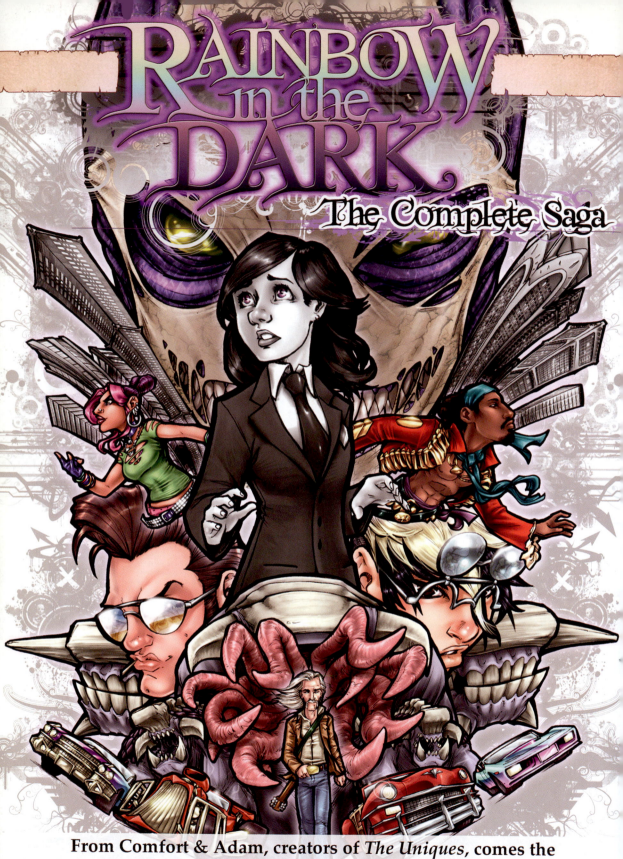